Peppa's Storybook Collection

This book is based on the TV series *Peppa Pig*. *Peppa Pig* is created by Neville Astley and Mark Baker.
Peppa Pig © Astley Baker Davies Ltd/Entertainment One UK Ltd 2003.

ISBN 978-1-338-21199-3

10 9 8 7 6 5 4 3 2 1   17 18 19 20 21
Printed in China   38

First printing 2017
www.peppapig.com
Book design by Jessica Meltzer

SCHOLASTIC INC.

Table of Contents

The Story of Peppa Pig

Once upon a time, there was a lovable, slightly bossy little piggy named Peppa.

Snort!

Grunt! Grunt!

More than anything in the whole wide world,
Peppa loved jumping UP and DOWN in muddy puddles.

Mummy Pig was Peppa's mommy. She was *very* wise about most things.

Mummy Pig would say, "Peppa, when you jump in muddy puddles, you must wear your boots."

Squelch! Squelch!

Daddy Pig was Peppa's daddy. He loved eating cookies, and he had a big, round tummy. When Daddy Pig jumped in muddy puddles, he made a very **big** muddy splash.

Ho, ho, ho!

splash!

When Peppa's little brother, George, was born, Peppa helped look after him.

And as soon as George was old enough, Peppa taught him how to jump in muddy puddles.

"George!" Peppa said, just like Mummy Pig. "If you jump in muddy puddles, you must wear your boots."

Squelch!

Squelch!

George liked muddy puddles, but he liked his toy
Mr. Dinosaur more. Even though George couldn't
speak yet, he could say one word *very* well . . .

Dine-saw!

Grrr!

Sometimes Peppa got a little bit annoyed with George. "George," she would sigh, "why do you ALWAYS say dine-saw for everything? It's soooo boring!"

One day, Peppa, George, Mummy, and Daddy Pig got into their little car and drove to their new house on top of a little green hill.

Peppa was excited about the new house, but she was very excited about the very wet and extremely muddy puddles in the yard!

BeeP! BeeP!

"Can we go and jump in the muddy puddles?"
asked Peppa.

"It's nearly time for bed, Peppa," replied Mummy.

"You'll have to wait until tomorrow."

Peppa and George woke up very early the next morning and went to find Mummy and Daddy Pig.

Hee! Hee! Hee!

Hee! Hee! Hee!

"Can we *please* go outside and jump in muddy puddles?" asked Peppa excitedly.

Snort! Snort!

Yaaawwwn!

"We're going to Granny and Grandpa Pig's house today, Peppa," replied Mummy Pig sleepily. "You can jump in muddy puddles there."

BeeP!

BeeP!

Snort!
Snort!

After breakfast, it was time to leave, so Peppa
and her family jumped into their little car.
"Ready?" asked Daddy Pig cheerily.
"Yes, Daddy Pig!" everyone answered back.
"Then, let's **GO!**" shouted Daddy Pig.

"Yippee!" cried Peppa. She couldn't wait to get to Granny and Grandpa Pig's house and jump in muddy puddles.

The family soon arrived at Granny and Grandpa's house. Peppa and George were very excited. They loved going to visit Granny and Grandpa Pig.

Granny Pig! Grandpa Pig!

Gangy Ig! Baba Ig!

"Granny Pig, Grandpa Pig!" cried Peppa.
"Gangy Ig, Baba Ig!" shouted George.
"Hello, my little ones!" answered Granny Pig. "Come inside."
"Granny," said Peppa. "Can I jump in muddy puddles please?"

"I think Grandpa Pig has something to show you first,
Peppa," said Granny Pig. Peppa was a little disappointed.
She really wanted to jump in muddy puddles.

Grandpa Pig took Peppa and George to his vegetable garden.

"This is where I grow my vegetables," said Grandpa Pig. "First I plant some seeds. . . ."

"Can we eat your yummy vegetables, Grandpa?" asked Peppa, forgetting all about muddy puddles.

"We have to wait for them to grow a bit bigger," replied Grandpa.

"Ooooooh!" gasped Peppa excitedly.

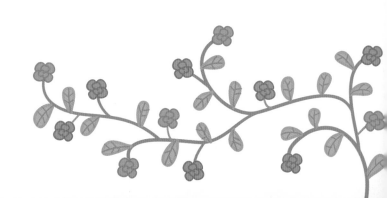

21

Suddenly, there was a loud **BANG!**
"Oh, dear!" gasped Grandpa Pig. "That was thunder. That means it's going to rain. We should hurry inside before we get wet."

Peppa, George, and Grandpa Pig ran inside as fast as they could to get out of the rain.

Peppa and George
watched the rain
splish-splash-splosh
down the window.
George started to cry.
"Don't cry, George,"
said Peppa. "It's only rain."

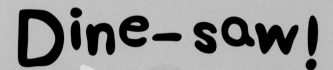

Dine-saw!

But George wasn't crying because it was raining.
George was crying because he had *lost* Mr. Dinosaur.

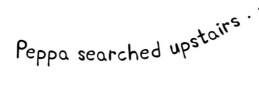

Peppa searched upstairs . . .

downstairs . . .

and even in the toilet . . .

but she couldn't find Mr. Dinosaur anywhere.
Just then, she had an idea. . . .

Peppa ran outside and found a *very* wet Mr. Dinosaur in Grandpa's *very* muddy vegetable garden.

She ran inside and gave Mr. Dinosaur to George. George was very happy.

Dine-saw! Grrr!

"The rain has stopped," cried Peppa. "What can we do now?"
"I have a very good idea, Peppa," said Daddy Pig, pointing outside.

"Hooray!" cheered Peppa, seeing the muddiest puddles ever.
Peppa had been so busy looking at Grandpa's vegetables
and searching for Mr. Dinosaur, she had forgotten all
about jumping in puddles.

Grunt!
Grunt!

Squelch!

Squelch!

Peppa loved jumping up and down in muddy puddles more than anything in the whole wide world. All of Peppa's family loved jumping up and down in muddy puddles more than anything in the whole wide world.

Snort! Snort!

Squelch!

Hee! Hee! Ha! Ha! Oink! Oink!

Hee! Hee! Hee! Ha! Ha! Grunt! Snort!

Best Friends

Once upon a time, Peppa's best friend,
Suzy Sheep, came to play.
"I have something to show you,"
said Suzy.

Suzy held up a photograph of a baby sheep. "Look! It's me," said Suzy.

"You're not a baby, Suzy," said Peppa, shaking her head.

"This is an **old** photo," Suzy explained.
"It was taken when I was a baby."

Peppa snorted. She didn't remember
Suzy being a baby. That was
just silly!

Suzy pointed at Peppa. "In the olden days you were a baby, too!" she said.

"I don't **remember** being a baby!" said Peppa.

"But you were," insisted Suzy. "Ask your **mummy**."

Peppa and Suzy raced inside. Mummy Pig was working on the computer.

"Mummy!" cried Peppa. "Suzy is making up stories."

"No, I'm not," Suzy said.

Peppa told Mummy Pig about Suzy's silly idea. "I don't remember being a baby!" Peppa insisted.

"But you **were** a baby, Peppa!" said Mummy Pig.

Mummy Pig pulled up a picture of a baby pig on the computer.

"Who do you think this is, Peppa?" she asked.

Peppa thought that the baby looked like her cousin, Baby Alexander.

"Is it Baby Alexander?" she asked.

"No," replied Mummy Pig.
"That's **YOU** as a baby,
Peppa!"
  Peppa was surprised. She
had been a baby!

Peppa and Suzy giggled.
Baby Peppa looked very cute!

George and Daddy Pig came in to see what all the fuss was about.

"Look, Daddy!" said Peppa. "That's me as a baby!"

"I remember it," said Daddy Pig. "That photo was taken on our first day in this house."

"What do you mean?" asked Peppa.

Daddy Pig told Peppa, Suzy, and George that they had moved into their house when Peppa was very little.

"We brought all our things on the top of our car," he said.

"Mummy Pig put up some pictures," said Daddy Pig.

"Daddy Pig put up a shelf," said Mummy Pig.

"And Grandpa Pig made us a lovely flower garden!"

Peppa and Suzy went outside. There was no flower garden at this house.

"Why don't we have a flower garden now?" Peppa asked.

"We used to. But Daddy Pig looked after it." Mummy Pig sighed.

"Um . . ." said Daddy Pig, embarrassed. "We had the wrong kind of soil for flowers."

"Was Suzy my friend in the olden days?" asked Peppa. Daddy Pig nodded. "Of course!" he said.

Hee!

Hee!

"You and Suzy have always been **best friends.**"

Peppa wondered what games she played with Suzy when they were little.

"Did we **jump** up and down in muddy puddles?" she asked.

"No." Mummy Pig laughed. "You were babies. You couldn't even walk yet!"

"What did we do when we were babies?" asked Suzy.

"You cried . . .

you burped . . .

and you laughed!"
said Mummy Pig.

Suzy and Peppa giggled. It must have been so silly being babies!

Hee! Hee!

Hee! Hee!

"Baby Peppa!"

"Baby Suzy!"

"Then you grew into toddlers," continued Mummy Pig.
"And you played together all the time."
"But where was George?" Peppa asked.

"He was a baby in my
tummy!"
said Mummy Pig.

Peppa thought for a moment. Daddy Pig's tummy was even bigger than Mummy's. "Is there a baby in there?" she asked. "No, Peppa," chuckled Daddy Pig.

"This tummy is **pure muscle!**"

51

"Soon, George was born," Mummy Pig said. "And Granny and Grandpa Pig brought him a very special present. Can you guess what it was, Peppa?"

Peppa knew just what present it must have been.

"Mr. Dinosaur!"

she cried.

53

Daddy Pig said that little Peppa and Suzy liked to do everything together!

They liked to **jump...**

Hee!

Hee!

La la la!

...a muddy

puddle!"

"You loved jumping up and down in muddy puddles together!" said Mummy Pig.

Peppa, George, and Suzy all ran outside.
"I still love muddy puddles!" cried Peppa.
"Me, too!" cried Suzy.

Peppa, George, and Suzy looked for the biggest muddy
puddle they could find and jumped right in!

Daddy Pig brought his camera. "Let's take a photo of you, Suzy, and George now, Peppa," he said.

"Yes!" exclaimed Peppa. "Because Suzy and I were best friends in the olden days. And we're still **best friends** now!"

Click!

Little or big, Peppa and Suzy will always be best friends. And they will always love jumping up and down in

muddy puddles!

George Catches a Cold

Mummy Pig says Peppa and George can play in the rain, but they must wear rain clothes to keep dry.

But George hates wearing his rain hat,
so he has thrown it in a muddy puddle.
Peppa knows that is not a good idea.

Hee, hee!

Snort!
Grunt!

"Come inside, children," calls Daddy Pig.
"It's raining too hard now."
"Where's your hat, George?" asks
Mummy Pig.
"Atchoo!" replies George.

Oh, dear. George has caught a cold.

"AAAATCHOOOOO!"

George cannot stop sneezing.
"Poor little George," says
Mummy Pig. "You don't look very well."
"Don't worry. I'll call Doctor Brown Bear,"
says Daddy Pig.

"Will George go to the hospital?" asks Peppa.
"No, George has to go to bed," replies Daddy.
"So George is not truly sick then,"
says Peppa, disappointed.

"George, you have to stay in bed until you are better," says Daddy Pig.

"Why?" asks George.

"Because you have to keep warm," says Daddy.

Doctor Brown Bear is here to see George.
"Open wide and say ahhhh," he says.
George is a little afraid of Doctor Brown Bear.
He hides under his sheets with Mr. Dinosaur.

Doctor Brown Bear asks Peppa to show George that he does not have to be scared.

"Ahhhh," says Peppa.

George laughs and comes out from under his sheets. He opens his mouth so Doctor Brown Bear can look.

"Ahhh," says George.

"George has caught a cold," Doctor Brown Bear
tells Mummy Pig. "He can have some warm milk at
bedtime to help him sleep."
"Thank you, Doctor Brown Bear!" says Mummy Pig.

"You're welcome. Good-bye!" says Doctor Brown Bear, before driving off in his special white car.

The next morning, George wakes up early. The warm milk made him sleep very well.

"*Roar!*" cries George, waking up Peppa. He is feeling much better.

Roar!

Hee, hee, hee!

It's a lovely sunny day but George is wearing his rain hat. He doesn't want to catch another cold.

"Oh, George! You don't need to wear your hat when it is warm and sunny!" Mummy Pig tells him.

"Hee, hee, hee!" everyone laughs.

George never goes in the rain without his hat again.

Princess Peppa

It is bedtime for Peppa and George. Mummy Pig tucks them in and turns out the light. "Good night, little piggies," she whispers.

Downstairs, Granny and Grandpa Pig arrive to have dinner with Mummy and Daddy Pig.

They all sit down to eat—but suddenly, they hear noises coming from upstairs! "Is that Peppa and George?" asks Grandpa Pig.
Looks like the little piggies aren't sleeping after all.

Mummy Pig goes upstairs to check on Peppa and George. They are wide-awake!

"Peppa! George! Quickly now, hop into bed," says Mummy Pig. "You're making lots of noise, and it's too late for you to be up."

"We aren't sleepy yet," says Peppa.

91

"Will you tell us a story?" asks Peppa. "We promise to go to sleep after a story!"

"All right," says Mummy Pig. "Once upon a time there was—"
"A princess!" Peppa jumps in.

"Oh, yes," says Mummy Pig. "Once upon a time, there was a courageous princess named Peppa. She lived in a castle with Sir George, the Brave Knight."

95

"And the princess and the knight had a cook who made the most delicious food ever," adds Peppa.
"Of course," says Mummy Pig. "She made cupcakes and cookies—"

97

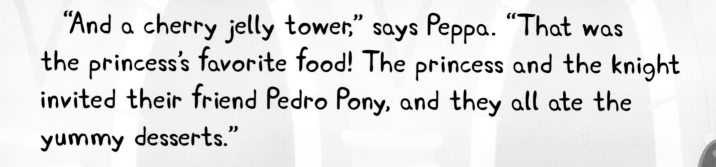

"And a cherry jelly tower," says Peppa. "That was the princess's favorite food! The princess and the knight invited their friend Pedro Pony, and they all ate the yummy desserts."

"Yes," says Mummy Pig. "And afterward, everyone was so full, they fell right asleep. The end."

"Then they woke up," cries Peppa. "And they invited
a wizard to the castle!"

"A wizard?" asks Mummy Pig.

"Yes," says Peppa. "And he did a big magic show!
But then, all of a sudden . . .

". . . A big green dragon came to the castle!" Peppa continues.

"Hee, hee, hee!" laughs George. "Grrr!"
"Oh, no!" says Mummy Pig. "How scary!"

"The dragon wasn't scary," says Peppa. "He was just very hungry! So the king came and ordered the cook to make a picnic," says Peppa.

"He did?" Mummy Pig asks with a yawn.

"Yes," says Peppa. "The cook, the wizard, the princess, the knight, the king, Pedro Pony, and the dragon sat down to a big feast."

"And then they went to sleep?" murmurs Mummy Pig as her head droops to one side. "No," says Peppa. "Then they had a party!"

"The princess arrived to the party in a beautiful carriage," says Peppa. "She came with her friend Suzy Sheep. Sir George pulled the carriage with his horse."

"All of their friends came to the castle to dance. There was Rebecca Rabbit and Pedro Pony and Danny Dog . . ."

Hee, hee, hee!

Downstairs, Daddy Pig, Granny Pig, and Grandpa Pig are wondering what is taking Mummy Pig so long. "Maybe we should see what's going on upstairs!" says Daddy Pig.

"I think I hear snoring," says Granny Pig. "Mummy Pig must have finally gotten Peppa and George to fall asleep!"

But Peppa and George are not snoring—Mummy Pig is!

Hee, hee, hee!

"It looks like Princess Peppa is the best at telling bedtime stories," says Daddy Pig.

George's New Dinosaur

George's favorite toy is Mr. Dinosaur.

George likes bouncing Mr. Dinosaur in the garden, playing with him at bath time, and cuddling with him when he goes to sleep.

At bedtime Peppa says, "George, I think Mr. Dinosaur is broken!"

George is very upset.
Mummy and Daddy
Pig come in to see why
George is crying.
"Poor George," says
Daddy Pig. "Maybe
it's time you got
a new dinosaur."

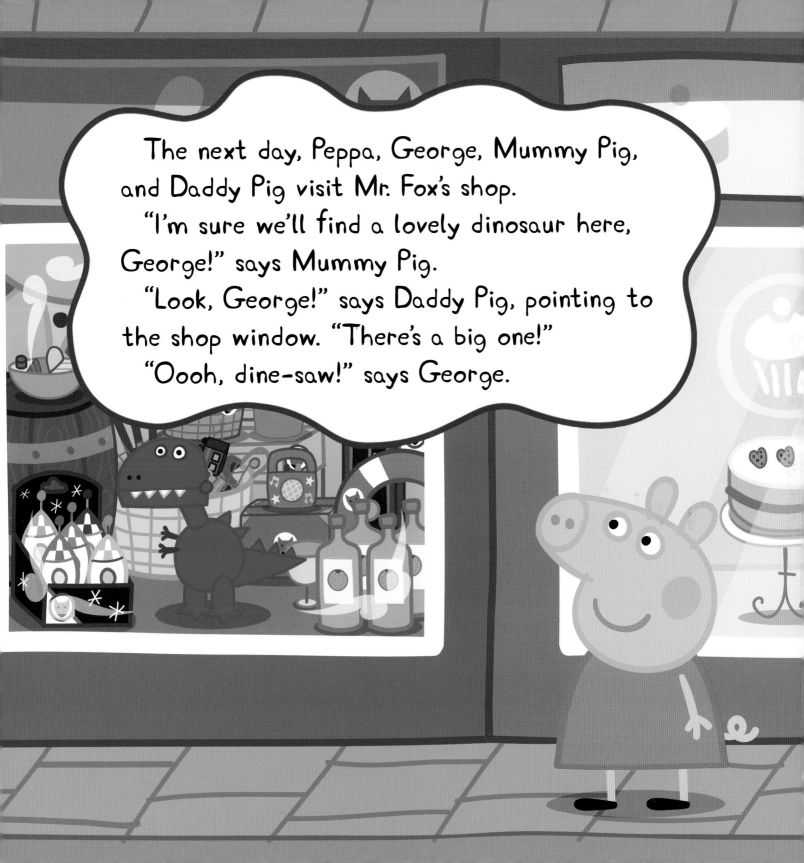

The next day, Peppa, George, Mummy Pig, and Daddy Pig visit Mr. Fox's shop.

"I'm sure we'll find a lovely dinosaur here, George!" says Mummy Pig.

"Look, George!" says Daddy Pig, pointing to the shop window. "There's a big one!"

"Oooh, dine-saw!" says George.

"Good morning!" says Mr. Fox. "Can I help you?"

"We'd like to buy the dinosaur in the window, please," says Daddy Pig.

"Good choice!" says Mr. Fox. "This is Dino-Roar. He walks, he talks, and he sings!"

"Dino-ROAR!" says George.

"We'll take it!" says Daddy Pig.

George is playing with Dino-Roar in the garden.

Dino-Roar sings, "Dino-Roar, Dino-Roar! Listen to Dino-Roar! *Roooooaaaaaaaaar!*"

"Careful, George," says Daddy Pig. "Don't play too roughly because Dino-Roar will break."

George wants to play with Dino-Roar in the bath.

Splash, Splash, SPLASH!

"Dino-ROAR!" says George.
Mummy Pig says, "George, if you get
Dino-Roar wet he'll stop working."

Peppa and George are asleep in bed. But suddenly Dino-Roar comes to life!

"Listen to Dino-Roar! *Roooaaar!*"

"George!" says Peppa. "Dino-Roar has woken me up!"

"Maybe Dino-Roar should sleep somewhere else," says Daddy Pig, taking Dino-Roar away.

George is feeling sad. He cannot play with Dino-Roar in the garden, or the bath, or even in bed.

"Don't worry, George," says Mummy Pig brightly. "Dino-Roar can still roar."

"Dino-Roar! Li . . . sten to Dino-Roo . . . aarr." Dino-Roar stops walking and talking completely.

"I think the batteries must have run out," says Mummy Pig.

"Already? How many are there?" grumbles Daddy Pig as batteries pour out of Dino-Roar. "Hundreds and thousands!" cries Peppa.

Suddenly, Peppa spots something green under a bush.

"What's this?" says Peppa. "Is it a trumpet?"

"You've found Mr. Dinosaur's tail," says Mummy Pig. "Now Daddy Pig can fix him."

"He might be a bit difficult to fix," says Daddy Pig doubtfully.

But the tail slips perfectly into place.
"Ho ho ho," chuckles Daddy Pig.
"Hello, Mr. Dinosaur," says Peppa.
"Dine-saw!" says George.

Click!

George is so happy to have his favorite toy back!

Grrr!

Peppa's First Sleepover

Peppa is going to her very first sleepover at
Zoe Zebra's house. "Welcome to my sleepover!"
Zoe says.

"I'll pick you up in the morning," Mummy Pig tells Peppa with a kiss. "Have fun!"

Rebecca Rabbit, Suzy Sheep, and Emily Elephant are already there. "I have my teddy," Peppa says.

Zoe has her monkey. Rebecca has her carrot.
Suzy has her owl. And Emily has her frog.

Mummy Zebra dims the lights in the living room.
"Don't stay up too late, girls! And don't be too loud.
Daddy Zebra has to get up early to deliver the mail."

Zoe's baby twin sisters, Zuzu and Zaza,
want to join the sleepover.
"Sleepovers are for big girls only!" Zoe says.

The twins begin to cry.
"They're so sweet and little," Peppa says.

WAAAH!

"Can they stay?" Rebecca asks.
"Okay," Zoe says to the twins. "But you
must promise NOT to fall asleep."

"What should we do first?" Suzy asks.
"I'm taking piano lessons!
Listen . . ." Zoe starts to pound
on the keys. "Twinkle, twinkle,
little star . . ."

Mummy Zebra has woken up.
"*Shush!* You must be quiet so Daddy Zebra can sleep!
Now, into your sleeping bags, please."

Snort! "What do we do now?" Peppa asks.

"At sleepovers, there's always a midnight feast!" Zoe says.

"It's when we eat things," Suzy says in a hushed voice, "in *secret*."

"Shhh!" Zoe whispers. She quietly leads the girls to the kitchen.
As they walk, the floorboards creak . . .

creak!

creak!

creak!

creak! creak!

Oh, no! The noise has woken Mummy Zebra up again. "Girls, you'll wake Daddy Zebra! Now, who knows a bedtime story?"

The girls take turns telling a story.

"Once upon a time, there was a little fairy . . ." Suzy begins.

"And she lived in the forest . . ." Peppa continues.

"And the fairy met a big monster, who went . . . RAARRR!" Emily makes a big elephant trumpet noise!

Oh, dear. The noise has woken Daddy Zebra!
"Sorry, Daddy," Zoe says. "There was a story
about a fairy and a scary monster."

"And we want to know what happens next!"
Peppa says.
"Very well," Daddy Zebra says. "The monster
lifted up his great, big hairy paws . . .

"And walked along on his great, big hairy feet . . . and sang . . . 'Twinkle, twinkle, little star, how I wonder what you are . . .'"

Daddy Zebra sings gently as he plays the piano. Soon, his song has sent everyone to sleep.

What a wonderful first sleepover this has been.
Sweet dreams, Peppa!

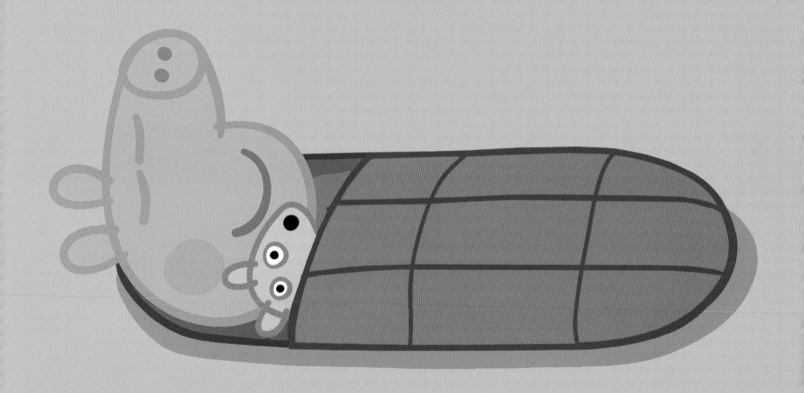

Playtime for Peppa and George

This is Peppa and George. Peppa is George's big sister. They share a bedroom and lots and lots of toys. Peppa and George love being brother and sister. They play fun games together every day!

Hee! Hee!

Grunt!

Snort!

One day, Peppa and George are with Mummy and Daddy Pig in the living room. Mummy Pig has to work on her computer and Daddy Pig wants to work in the garden.

"Peppa, George, why don't you two play a game?" asks Daddy Pig.

"Oh, goodie!" says Peppa. "George and I love to play games!"

"Snort, snort!" George likes that idea, too.

It is a lovely sunny day, so Peppa and George run outside.
"George, let's jump up and down in muddy puddles!"
shouts Peppa.

Splish
Splash!

But George does not want to jump in muddy puddles
today. He would like to play a different game.

"Okay," says Peppa. "We can play catch instead."
Peppa tosses a ball to George. But George does not
want to play catch, either.

"George, what *would* you like to play?" asks Peppa.

"Oink, oink!" George has an idea for a new game.

Peppa follows George to Mummy and Daddy Pig's bedroom.

"There's nothing fun to play in here," says Peppa.
George shows Peppa a box at the end of the bed.
"What's this?" asks Peppa.

"Wow!" says Peppa. "George, do you want to dress up and pretend to be Mummy and Daddy?"
"Oink, oink!" George does want to dress up!

"Good idea!" says Peppa. "I want to play that game, too!"

Peppa helps George put on Daddy Pig's black hat, coat, and shoes.

"Now, you must pretend to be *exactly* like Daddy Pig," she says.

George thinks for a moment.
"SNORT!" He makes a loud noise, just like Daddy Pig.
"Very good, George!" says Peppa. "Now it's my turn."

Peppa puts on Mummy Pig's fancy dress and hat. Then she puts on the high-heeled shoes. Suddenly, Peppa is very tall.

"Hee, hee, hee!" they giggle.

Dressing up is very silly!

"George, what else do I need to look *exactly* like
Mummy?" Peppa asks.
"Snort, snort!" George does not know.

Peppa goes over to Mummy Pig's dresser. Sometimes
Peppa watches Mummy Pig sit in front of the mirror and
get ready to go out with Daddy Pig.

"I need makeup, of course!" she says.

"First, some powder." Peppa pats the pink powder on her cheeks.

Puff, puff, puff!

"Lovely!"

"Now for some lipstick."

Peppa draws on a smile using Mummy's shiny red lipstick. "How do I look?"

"SNORT!" George thinks Peppa makes a very pretty Mummy Pig.

"Come along, Daddy Pig," says Peppa. "It's time to go to work."

Peppa and George walk downstairs.

They find the real Mummy Pig working on her computer.
"Hello, Peppa. Hello, George," says Mummy Pig.
"I beg your pardon," says Peppa. "I'm not Peppa. I'm
Mummy Pig. And this is Daddy Pig."

"Oh, I see," says Mummy Pig. "Hello, Mummy Pig. Hello, Daddy Pig."

"George," Peppa whispers. "Remember to act *exactly* like Daddy."

"SNORT!" says George.

"Excuse me," says Peppa. "I have a *lot* of work to do."

She picks up Mummy Pig's telephone. "Hello. Yes!
Do this, do that. Thank you!"

Then Peppa taps on the computer keyboard.
Tap! Tap! Tap!
Peppa is very good at pretending to be Mummy Pig.

alpc jfdslkjs da
a.kjdnkjasd vjsl
nnvlam nrdl
sjljdg

kas dplk jlbd

"All right. Good-bye!" she says, hanging up the phone.
"And, done! Come on, Daddy Pig. It's time you did some
work, too."

Peppa and George go back outside. They find Daddy Pig digging a hole in the garden. "Hello, Peppa and George," says Daddy Pig. "I'm not Peppa. I'm Mummy Pig. And this is Daddy Pig," says Peppa.

"Oh, I see," says Daddy Pig. "What are you up to today?"
"We are here to do some work," declares Peppa.
George jumps into the hole and begins to dig.
He is having fun pretending to work like Daddy Pig.

Peppa jumps into the hole to help George dig.
Suddenly, they hear Mummy Pig calling from the house.
"Peppa! George!"

Mummy Pig has brought ice cream for everyone.
"You must take off those muddy clothes before you eat,
Peppa and George," she says.
"Snort! I'm *Mummy Pig* and this is *Daddy Pig!*" Peppa
insists.

"Are you sure?" asks Mummy Pig. "That's a shame, because I have Peppa and George's favorite ice cream flavors. But if we can't find them . . ."

Peppa and George quickly take off the muddy clothes.
"Here we are!" shouts Peppa. "We were only pretending
to be you and Daddy Pig."

"Ho, ho! You really had us fooled," says Daddy Pig.
"It was George's idea to dress up," says Peppa.
"Oink!" George nods, licking his ice cream.
"You both did a very good job," says Mummy Pig.

Peppa and George love ice cream.
And they love pretending to be Mummy and Daddy Pig.
But most of all, they love being brother and sister.